ordinary
terrible
things

WITHDRAWN

ordinary
terrible
things

ordinary
terrible
things

DIVORCE IS THE WORST

Written and illustrated by
Anastasia Higginbotham

dottir
press
• NEW YORK CITY

Published in 2019 by Dottir Press
33 Fifth Avenue
New York, NY 10003

dottirpress.com

First published in 2015
Copyright © 2015 and 2019 by Anastasia Higginbotham

SECOND EDITION
First printing June 2019

Illustration and design by Anastasia Higginbotham
Photography by Alexa Hoyer | Production by Drew Stevens

Trade distribution by Consortium Book Sales and Distribution, www.cbsd.com.

Library of Congress Cataloging-in-Publication Data is available for this title.
ISBN 978-1-9483-4020-5

Manufactured in Malaysia by Tien Wah Press, April 2019

For the 5As,

Norman,

and JoAnn

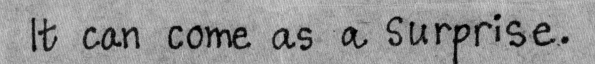

It can come as a surprise.

5

When it does,

6

You may feel confused,

or betrayed.

10

You may want to run.

You may be heartbroken.

15

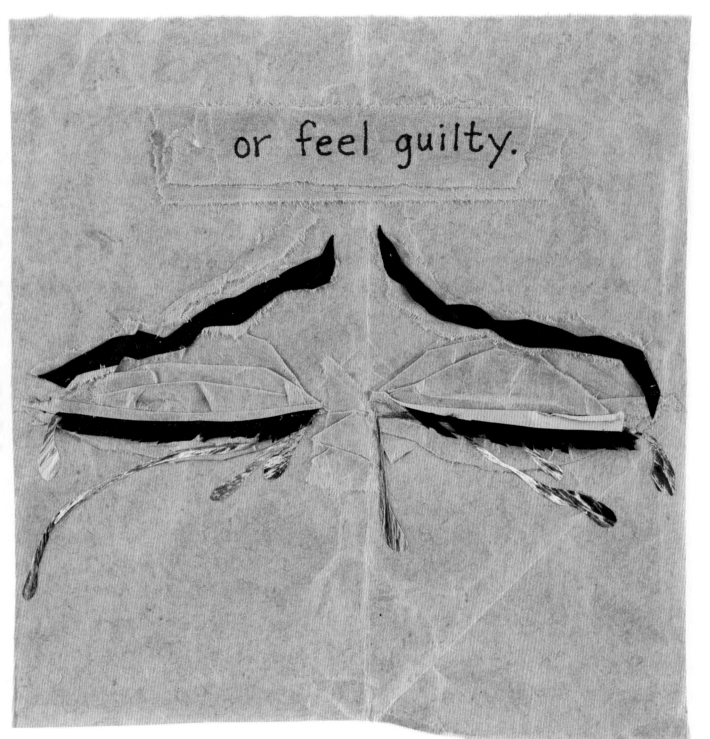

or feel guilty.

If you feel all of these ways
at once,

lie down.

We don't decide our parents' lives.

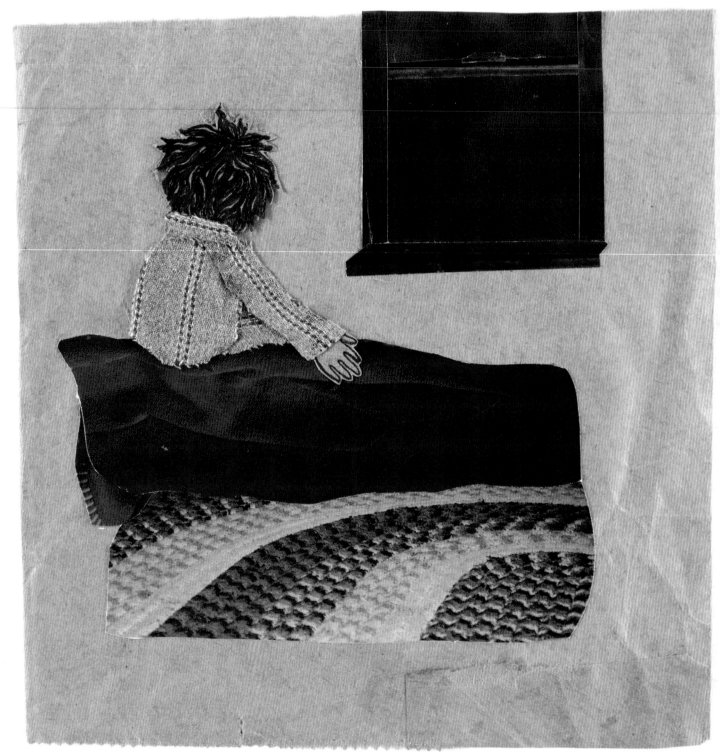

22

What they decide
affects our lives.

Divorce changes things.

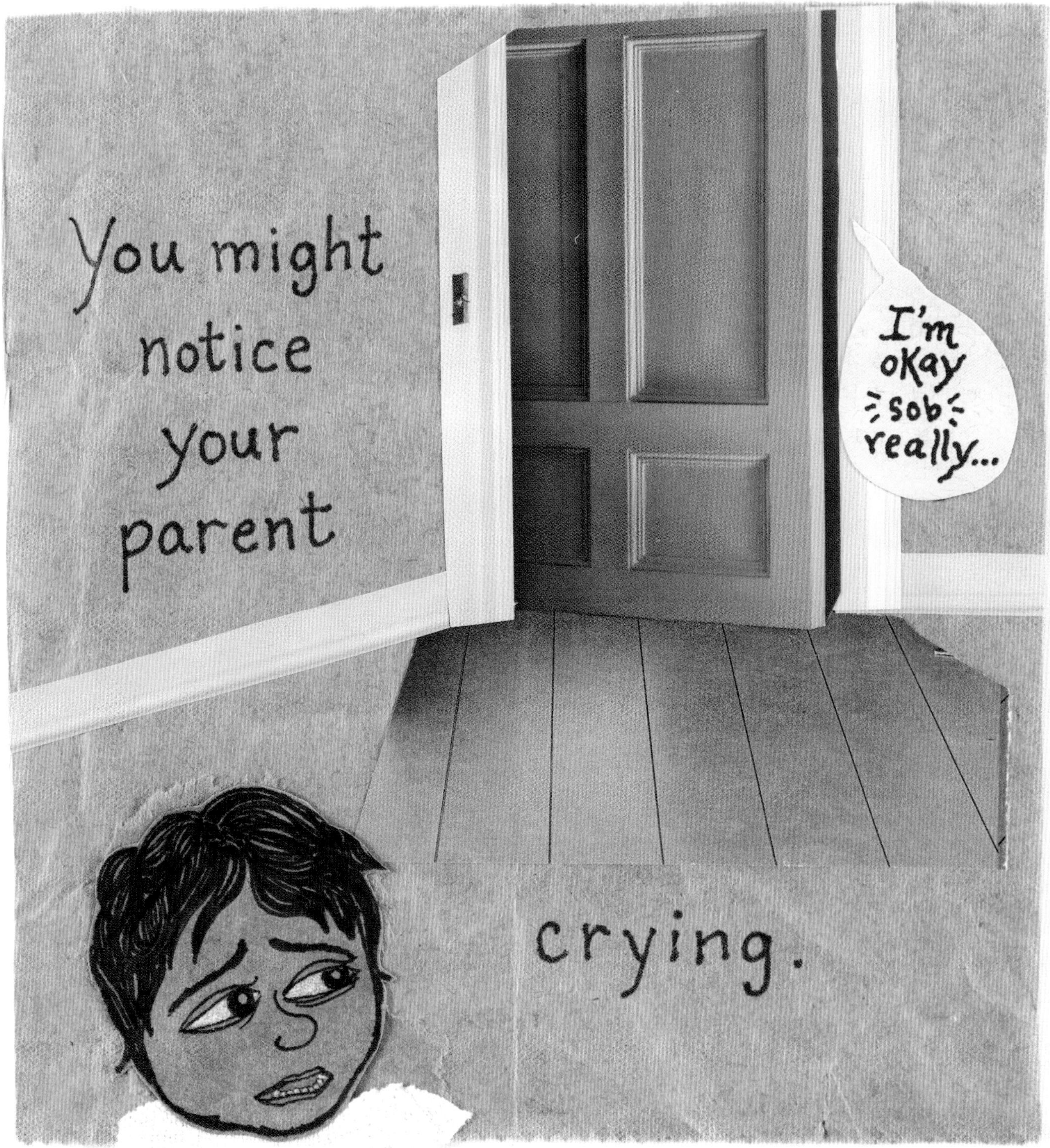
You might notice your parent
I'm okay sob really...
crying.

You might
notice them

26

This was NOT my idea, remember?!
Well, then you should have made different choices!
...not crying.

You might cry over little things.

You might not cry...

...over big things.

33

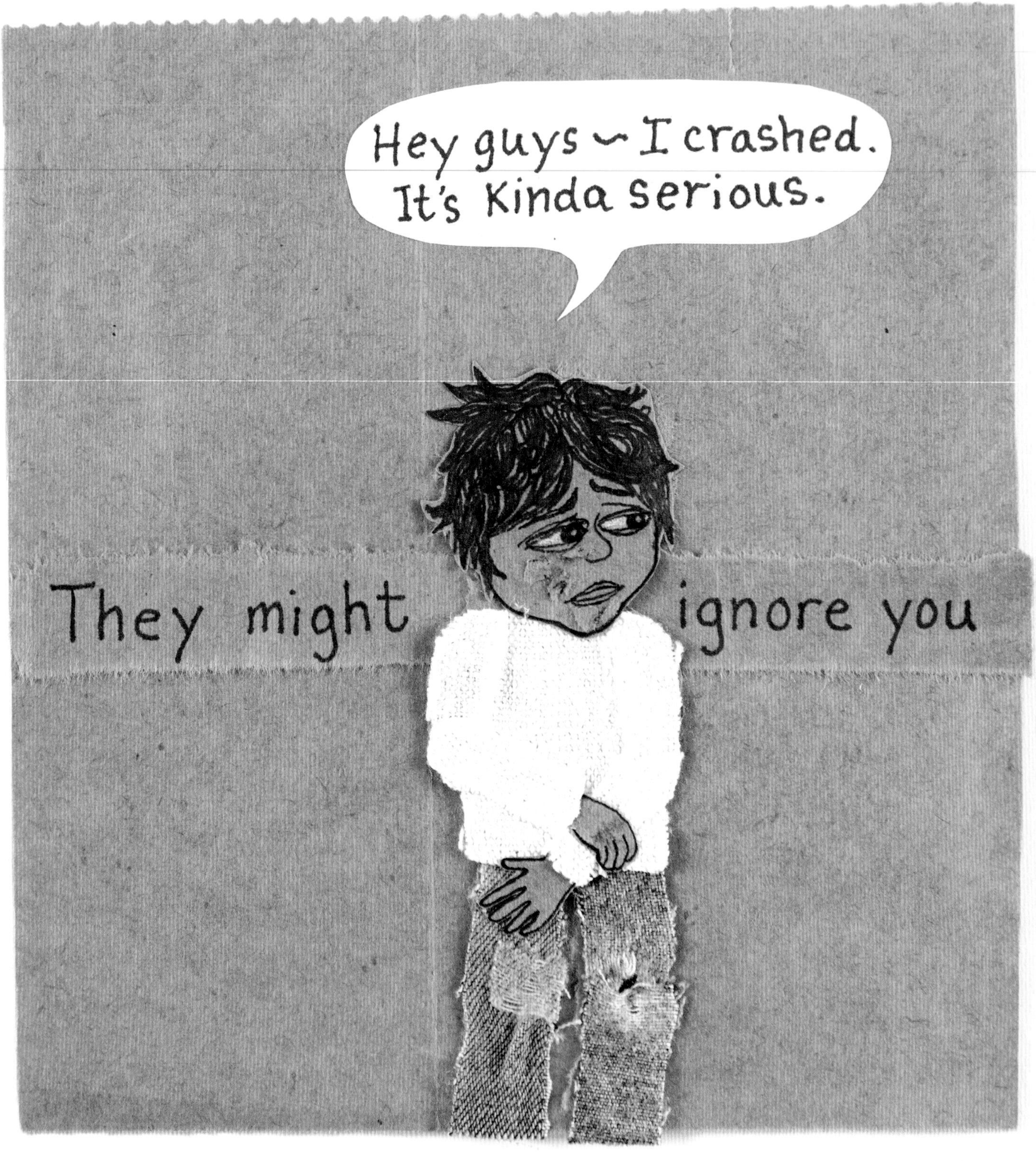
Hey guys ~ I crashed. It's Kinda serious.
They might ignore you

I made popcorn
if you want some.

without realizing it.

I hope you
remembered
to put your
bike away.

They might buy you outrageous gifts.

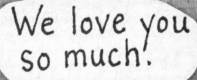

We love you so much!

And since your bike is wrecked...

37

Contrary to the title of this book, meeting a parent's ♥ *friend* ♥ is WORSE than the worst making it the **ABSOLUTE WORST**, even if the friend turns out to be nice, sort of, later on.

AAAAAAAH!!

They have their reasons.

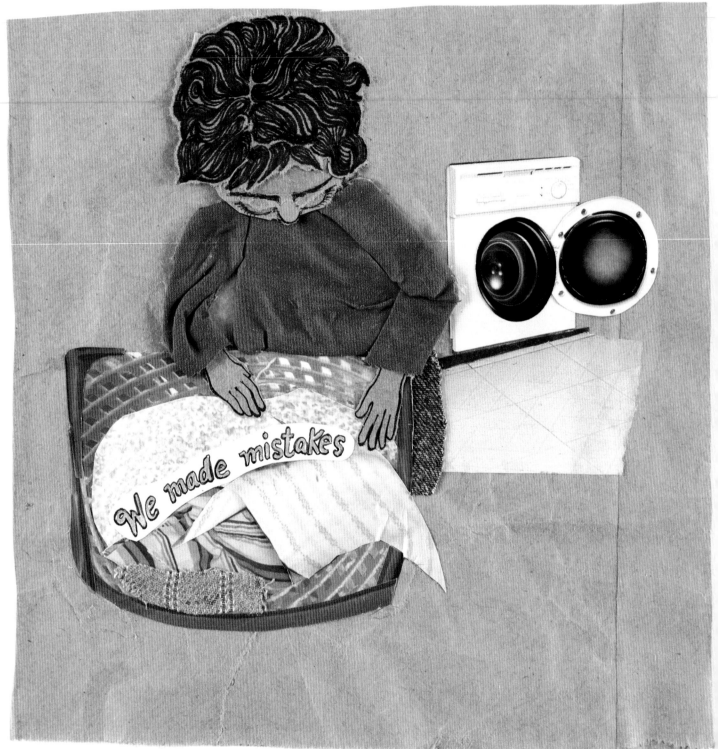

We've changed

44

Their reasons are theirs,
not yours.

45

When a parent
who used to be

like this

becomes more

like this,

Maybe a divorce is for the best
— for them.

You got your stuff
for the weekend?

Divorce can feel like being pulled in two directions at once.

Sometimes, exactly like that.

Divorce
means
your
parents

are splitting
from each other.

YOU

stay in one piece.

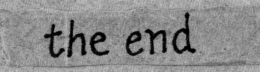

the end

Here is what to do with all those feelings and more:

Lay that burden down.

feel rejected by parent who moved out

wish I could sleep in my own real bed

there's someone new at breakfast

must love my parents more — so they won't be sad

no one pays attention to me

must fix my parents' lives

I'm worried about $$$

they're always working

Make a special place for them out of your way. Know your troubles as well as you can. Then let them be.

Use snips, scraps, and brown paper bags to make your pages and tell your own story!

You need a GLUE STICK

brown bag

catalogs

magazines

and

any image that was on its way to the trash

or recycling

You can do this activity even if your parents are together!

Start by creating a place where you can be all in one piece.

Choose a sky that mirrors what you feel.

Find trees to lift you up or hide you.
Trees bear witness and stand by you.

Choose the ground, rocks, roots, and grass that best support you.

And now you make **YOU:**

Dressed in scraps of clothes you've outgrown.

Hands

Head

Ribbon hair can be any way you like.

Anastasia Higginbotham's books about ordinary, terrible things tell stories of children who navigate trouble with their senses sharp and souls intact.

Help may come from family, counselors, teachers, and dreams — but it's the children who find their own way through.

Anastasia has been making books by hand her whole life as a way to cope with change and grow.

꒷ You CAN TOO! ꒦

ordinary
terrible
things

ordinary
terrible
things